Islands

Christopher Durbin

BLACKBIRCH®
PRESS

THOMSON

GALE

San Diego • Detroit • New York • San Francisco • Cleveland • New Haven, Conn. • Waterville, Maine • London • Munich

Geography First

Titles in this series
Coasts • Islands • Maps and Symbols
Mountains • Rivers and Streams • Volcanoes

THOMSON
*
GALE ™

© 2004 by White-Thompson Publishing Ltd.

Produced by White-Thompson Publishing Ltd.
2/3 St. Andrew's Place
Lewes BN7 1UP, U.K.

For more information, contact
The Gale Group, Inc.
27500 Drake Rd.
Farmington Hills, MI 48331-3535
Or you can visit our Internet site at http://www.gale.com

Geography consultant: John Lace, School Adviser
Editor: Katie Orchard
Picture research: Glass Onion Pictures
Designer: Chris Halls at Mind's Eye Design Ltd, Lewes
Artist: Peter Bull

Title page: The tropical islands of the Bahamas.
Contents page: Dense rain forest on St. Lucia.
Page 31: The Danish island of Stryno Kalv has only three farmhouses on it.

Originally published by Hodder Wayland,
an imprint of Hodder Children's Books,
a division of Hodder Headline Limited
338 Euston Road, London NW1 3BH

Acknowledgements:
The author and publisher would like to thank the following for their permission to reproduce the following photographs: Corbis 9 (Jay Dickman), 16 (Michael S. Lewis), 22 (Bojan Brecelj), 26 (Alan Schein Photography); Ecoscene 21 (Edward Bent), 24 (Stephen Coyne), 25 (Nick Hanna), 27 (PT); Hodder Wayland Picture Library *title page, chapter openers,* 18, 31; Natural Science Photos 17 (C. Dani and I. Jeske), 19 (I. Bennett); Oxford Scientific Films 5 (Kathie Atkinson), 7 (Ian West), 12 (Norbert Wu), 20 (Robin Bush); Popperfoto 11 (Reuters/Japan Coast Guard); Photodisc *cover;* Still Pictures 4 (Roger de la Harpe), 15 (Gerard and Margi Moss), 23 (Massimo Lupidi); Travel Ink 14 (Geraint Tellem), 28 (Patrick Ford).

LIBRARY OF CONGRESS CATALOGING-IN-PUBLICATION DATA

Durbin, Christopher.
 Islands / by Christopher Durbin.
  p. cm. — (Geography first)
Includes bibliographical references (p.) and index.
Contents: What is an island?—Rocky islands—Sand islands—Volcanic islands—Coral reef islands—Patterns of islands—Climates and sea levels—Island plants—Island animals—People and islands—Vacation islands—Big city islands—Island fact file.
 ISBN 1-4103-0111-7 (hardback:alk. paper)
1. Islands—Juvenile literature. [1. Islands.] I. Title. II. Series.

GB471.D87 2004
910'.914'2—dc22   2003016795

Printed in China
10 9 8 7 6 5 4 3 2 1

Words in bold **like this** are explained in the glossary on page 30.

Contents

What is an island?

An island is a piece of land surrounded by water. An island is smaller than a **continent** and larger than a rock. Most islands are found in oceans and seas, but some are found in lakes and rivers.

▼ Tiny rocky islands jut out of the sea around Pemba Island, off the coast of Tanzania.

There are many different types of islands. Some have hard, rocky **coasts.** Others have soft, sandy beaches.

Some islands, like Greenland, are very large. Others are very small and may have little **fresh water**. They are usually **uninhabited**, which means that no one lives on them.

▼ *Masthead Island is part of Australia's Great Barrier Reef. It is very small and has very little fresh water, so no one lives on it.*

Rocky islands

Some small, rocky islands are found just off the coast of a large piece of land, or **mainland**. They are usually made of very hard rock.

Over time, the sea **erodes**, or wears away, the softer rock on the mainland. A piece of hard rock may be left behind, forming an island.

How a Rocky Island Is Formed

A headland with soft and hard rock areas.

The sea erodes soft rock from both sides.

The sea breaks through, leaving a hard rock island and the mainland.

Some rocky islands can be reached at low **tide** when the sea goes out. The low-lying land between the island and the mainland is called a **causeway**. When the tide comes back in, the sea floods the causeway and separates the island from the mainland once more.

▼ *St. Michael's Mount in Cornwall, England. When the tide goes out, the causeway is revealed.*

Sand islands

Some islands are made of sand. They form in areas where the sea is shallow. Where the sea **currents** are not very strong, sand builds up slowly to form a **sandbank**. When the tide goes out, sandbanks can be seen as small sandy mounds.

From Sandbank to Island

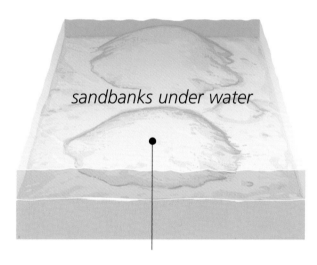

sandbanks under water

Sandbanks develop on the seabed.

The tide goes out and sandbanks are revealed. Wind blows more sand onto the shore, and sandbanks grow.

Sandbanks now remain above sea level even when the tide is in. The sandbanks are now islands.

Plants start to grow and sand is trapped, making the islands taller.

Wind blows sand onto the shore. This new sand makes the sandbanks even higher. When the tide comes in, a sandbank may remain out of the water, forming a sandy island. Grass grows on the island and traps more sand. This helps the island grow bigger.

▼ *A fishing boat sails around the Florida Keys, a group of sand islands.*

Volcanic islands

Some islands are formed by underwater **volcanoes**. Under the Earth's surface is a layer of hot, liquid rock, called **magma**. When magma breaks through the Earth's surface, or **erupts**, a volcano is formed.

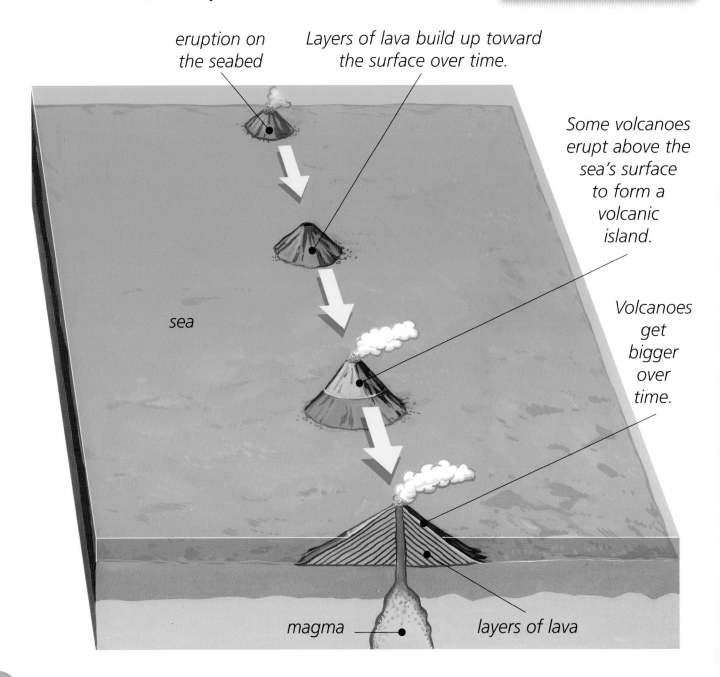

eruption on the seabed

Layers of lava build up toward the surface over time.

Some volcanoes erupt above the sea's surface to form a volcanic island.

Volcanoes get bigger over time.

sea

magma ———

layers of lava

When magma erupts, it is called **lava**. Under the sea, the hot lava cools down quickly to form a layer of solid rock.

Each time the volcano erupts, layers of lava gradually build up on top of one another. In this way, the volcano grows. Over time it breaks through the surface of the sea to form an island.

▼ *Smoke billows from the volcanic island of Torishima, in Japan.*

Coral reef islands

Most **coral reefs** are made by small animals that live only in warm, shallow seas. These animals live near the coast of an island.

▼ A diver explores a colorful coral reef in the Pacific Ocean.

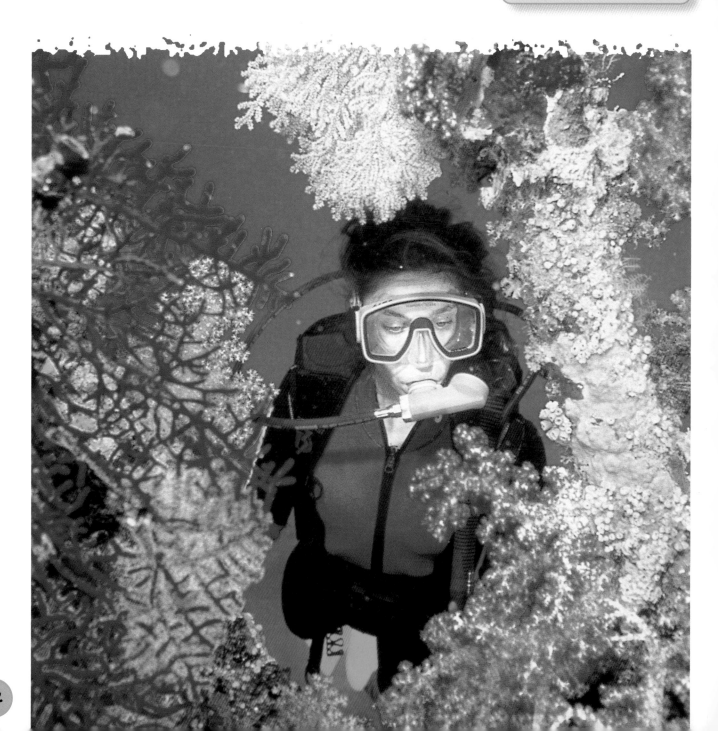

When the animals grow they leave behind **coral**, which is hard, like rock. Corals grow upwards towards the sea surface.

Many coral reefs form rings around volcanic islands. Over time, the volcano may sink or collapse. The coral island is left behind, with a **lagoon**, or pool, in the middle. This type of island is called an **atoll**.

volcano   coral reef   sinking volcano   reef grows toward the surface   ring-shaped island, or atoll   lagoon

A coral reef grows up in the warm, shallow water around a volcanic island.

The volcano sinks and the coral reef continues to grow.

The volcano disappears from sight, leaving the coral reef behind.

Patterns of islands

Islands can form in groups, or patterns. The most common pattern is a curved line of islands, called an **arc**. Usually, an island arc is a line of undersea volcanoes. Over time, the volcanoes erupt along a crack or weakness in the surface of the Earth and grow above sea level.

▼ *Oahu is one of many Hawaiian islands that make up an island arc, formed from undersea volcanoes.*

An **archipelago** is a group of small islands close together. They are usually found near coasts where the rocks are harder in some places than in others. The sea erodes the softer rock, leaving behind a group of hard rock islands.

▼ *These islands form part of the Juan Fernandez archipelago, which is near Chile.*

Climates and sea levels

Islands do not all have the same **climates**, or weather conditions. How hot or cold an island is depends on where it is in the world. Islands near the **Equator** are very warm. Those near the **North Pole** and **South Pole** may be covered with snow and ice all year.

▼ *Snow and ice cover this part of Greenland all year round.*

Sea levels rise and fall over many years. When the sea level falls, more of the sea bed around an island can be seen, and the island may become bigger. When the sea rises, islands may become flooded. Low-lying islands may disappear altogether.

▲ *As sea levels rise, some of these islands in French Polynesia may become smaller, or even disappear.*

Island plants

The plants growing on an island depend on its climate. On **Arctic** islands it is too cold for any trees to grow. Hot, dry, **desert** islands may have very few plants growing on them. Some wet and warm islands are completely covered with dense forest.

▼ *Dense rain forest grows on the island of St. Lucia in the British West Indies.*

At first, new islands have no plants growing on them. Then wind blows seeds onto an island from the mainland.

Grasses are usually the first plants to grow. Birds may fly in, bringing seeds in their droppings. Bushes and other plants will then grow from these seeds.

▼ *This Australian sandbank is only revealed at low tide. It does not yet have any plants growing on it.*

Island animals

Many islands are home to animals that are not found anywhere else. This is because they are **isolated**, or separate, from the mainland. Over time the animals that live there have had to **adapt**, or change, to cope with conditions on the island.

▼ *The kakapo is a rare flightless bird that lives on Stewart Island, New Zealand.*

Some islands used to have flightless birds and no **predators**. When people from Europe explored these islands hundreds of years ago, they brought with them cats and rats. The predators killed off many of the birds, which could not fly away.

▼ A marine iguana comes face to face with two booby birds on the Galápagos Islands.

People and islands

Many people live and work on islands. For most islanders, living on an island is the same as living anywhere else.

On some **remote** islands, it is expensive to transport goods and food from other countries. The land may have to be carefully farmed to grow food for the people on the island.

▲ These men are loading a sailing boat in Zanzibar with cargo. The boat takes goods from the mainland to islands in the Indian Ocean.

On many small islands, fishing is an important industry. Much of the fish is sold to islanders, or to restaurants and supermarkets. The rest is sold to other countries.

▼ *Fishermen sort through their catch on the coast of Iceland. Iceland is the third-largest fishing nation in Europe.*

Vacation islands

Many people from places with cool or wet climates visit warm islands for a vacation. Tourists enjoy the sun, sea, and beautiful scenery. Millions of people from Northern Europe fly to islands in the Mediterranean Sea. People from North America often choose the Caribbean islands.

▼ *Thousands of tourists visit the tropical island of Sri Lanka each year. These visitors have come to see baby elephants at an elephant orphanage.*

If islands become too popular, they can become overcrowded. Litter and building work can damage the beautiful **environment** people have come to see.

▲ *High-rise hotels line Waikiki Beach in Hawaii. Tourists go there for the white sandy beaches and warm sea.*

Big city islands

Some islands are located where rivers meet the sea. In the past, these were good places for people to settle. People living there could travel to and from faraway places. Some of these islands became **ports**. People came to buy and sell goods, and big cities grew.

▼ *Manhattan Island is the city center of New York. More than 1 million people live there.*

When people build cities on islands, they run out of land for building, so the buildings are often very tall.

In some places large amounts of earth and rocks are pushed into the sea to make new flat land to build on. This is called reclaimed land.

▼ *Hong Kong has 7,394,000 people living on 422 square miles (1,092 sq km). Many of its buildings stand on land reclaimed from the sea.*

Island fact file

1. The largest island in the world is Greenland, at 840,004 square miles (2,175,000 sq km). It is mainly made up of mountains covered with snow and ice.

2. The second-largest island is New Guinea.

3. Java, Indonesia (below), has the highest island population at 120 million. Indonesia is made up of more than 13,000 islands.

4. The smallest island that is a country is Nauru, in the Pacific Ocean. The whole island is only 7.72 square miles (20 sq km).

5. Manitoulin Island in Lake Huron, Canada, is the largest island in a lake.

6. The world's most remote island with people living on it is Tristan da Cunha. It is about 1,739 miles (2,800 km) west of South Africa and about the same distance east of South America.

7. One of the newest islands is part of Tonga in the Pacific Ocean. The island was formed when an undersea volcano erupted in June 1995.

8. Tebua Tarawa and Abanuea, two South Pacific islands in Kiribati, disappeared in 1999 as sea levels rose to new heights.

9 The island country most at risk from sea level rise is the Maldives in the Indian Ocean. The highest point is just over 6.5 feet (2 m) above sea level.

10 The name of the Lakshadweep Islands, off south-west India, means "100,000 islands." There are only 27!

The World's Major Island Groups

Numbers on this map refer to numbers in the fact file.

Glossary

Adapt Change in some way.

Arc A curved line.

Archipelago A group of islands.

Arctic The area around the North Pole.

Atoll A ring-shaped island made from a coral reef, surrounding a volcanic island.

Causeway A road that is covered by the sea at high tide.

Climate The normal weather for an area of the world.

Coast The place where land meets the sea.

Continent A continuous area of land, usually containing several countries.

Coral A hard, rocklike substance built up by animals in warm seas.

Coral reef A bank of coral, where lots of tropical fish swim.

Currents Strong, underwater movements of the sea.

Desert An area of land with a dry climate. It can be sandy or rocky.

Environment The natural surroundings of an area.

Equator An imaginary line around the middle of the Earth.

Erode Wear away.

Erupt When magma, gases, and ash are forced through the surface of the Earth.

Fresh water Drinking water. Sea water contains salt and cannot be drunk by humans.

Isolated Cut off from anywhere else.

Lagoon A saltwater lake or shallow sea surrounded by a coral island.

Lava Molten rocks that erupt from volcanoes.

Magma Hot, liquid rock that is found under the Earth's surface.

Mainland The main area of a continent or a country, not the islands around it.

North Pole The point on the globe that is farthest north.

Port A place where ships load and unload the goods that they carry.

Predator An animal that hunts other animals.

Remote Far away.

Sandbank A bank of sand underwater or above sea level.

South Pole The point on the globe that is farthest south.

Tide The rising and falling of the sea.

Uninhabited A place without people living there.

Volcano A place where lava, ash, and gases erupt from beneath the Earth's surface.

For more information

Durbin, Christopher. *Volcanoes.* San Diego: Blackbirch, 2004.

Green, Jen. *A Coral Reef.* New York: Crabtree, 2002.

Mattern, Joanne. *Greenland: World's Largest Island.* New York: Rosen, 2003.

Morris, Neal, and Ann Morris. *Earth's Changing Islands.* Austin, TX: Raintree, 2004.

Sheppard, Charles. *Coral Reefs.* Stillwater, MN: Voyageur Press, 2002.

Winne, Joanne. *Living on an Island.* New York: Welcome Books, 2000.

Index

All the numbers in **bold** refer to photographs and illustrations as well as text.